Agenda

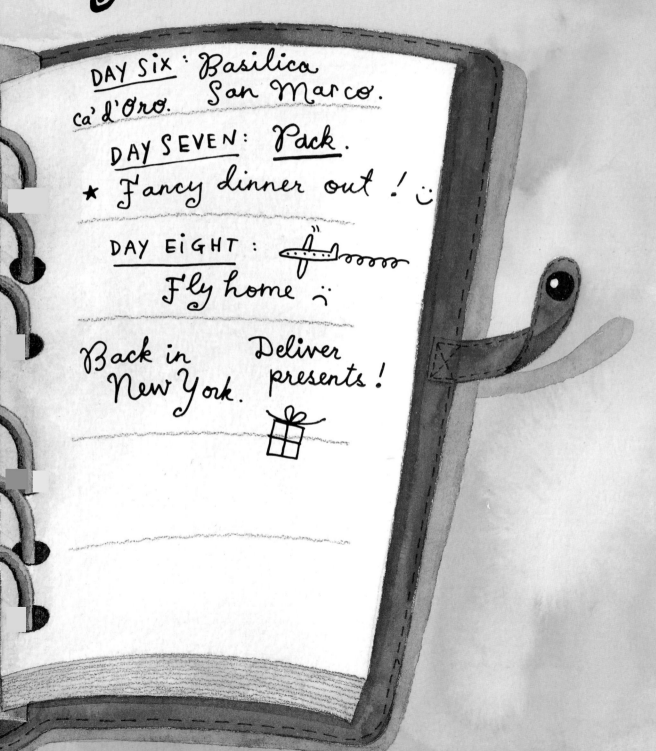

DAY SIX : Basilica
Ca' d'Oro.   San Marco.

DAY SEVEN : Pack.
★ Fancy dinner out ! ☺

DAY EIGHT : ✈~~~~~
Fly home ☹

Back in   Deliver
New York. presents !

For Zoe and Doris, who inspired this book; for my parents,
who made it all possible; and for Mickey — Claudia Mauner

To Robert, William and Matthew with all my love — Elisa Smalley

Our thanks to Doris Alexander, Meg Cabot, Joel Foster, Eleonora Riva
and Rosemary Stimola for their invaluable contributions to this book.

Text © 2003 by Claudia Mauner and Elisa Smalley.
Illustrations © 2003 by Claudia Mauner.

Book design by Kristine Brogno and Jessica Dacher.
Typeset in Filosofia.
The illustrations in this book were rendered in watercolor and india ink.
Manufactured in Hong Kong.

Library of Congress Cataloging-in-Publication Data
Mauner, Claudia.
Zoe Sophia's scrapbook : an adventure in Venice / by Claudia Mauner and Elisa Smalley ;
illustrated by Claudia Mauner.
p. cm.
Summary: Nine-year-old Zoe Sophia travels with Mickey, her dachshund, from
New York City to Venice, Italy, for a visit with a famous author—her aunt Dorothy.
ISBN 0-8118-3606-1
[1. Venice (Italy)—Fiction. 2. Voyages and travels—Fiction.
3. Aunts—Fiction. 4. Dachshunds—Fiction. 5. Dogs—Fiction.
6. Italy-Fiction.] I. Smalley, Elisa. II. Title.
PZ7.M44513 Zo 2003
[Fic]—dc21
2002009022

Distributed in Canada by Raincoast Books
9050 Shaughnessy Street, Vancouver, British Columbia V6P 6E5

10 9 8 7 6 5 4 3 2 1

Chronicle Books LLC
85 Second Street, San Francisco, California 94105

www.chroniclekids.com

Zoe Sophia's Scrapbook

An Adventure in Venice

By Claudia Mauner and Elisa Smalley · Illustrated by Claudia Mauner

chronicle books · san francisco

Riverside Drive, New York, N.Y., U.S.A.

My name is Zoe Sophia and I am nine years old. People tell me I'm wise for my age, even though I'm only four feet two. I live on the Upper West Side of Manhattan. The door to my building is easy to find because it has a big purple awning out front. The doorman is Victor Gonzales. He is a good friend of mine and has shiny gold buttons on his uniform coat, just like a palace guard. I love living in New York. There is so much to do here, like eating hot pretzels on the steps of the Metropolitan Museum of Art, trying on sunglasses at the Columbus Avenue flea market and walking my dachshund, Mickey, along Riverside Drive.

Tonight, 5:30 p.m.

Mickey and I love Manhattan, but traveling to faraway places is exciting, too. Tonight is super special because we are flying to Venice, Italy—Venezia—for the first time to visit my great aunt Dorothy Pomander, who is a writer. (That is what I want to be when I grow up.) D. P. is my very favorite person in the whole wide world. D. P. hasn't seen me in a while, so my mother gave me a red beret to wear, so I would be easy for her to spot. Mickey is wearing a silver tag on his collar with "Mickey, The Antwerp, Manhattan, New York" engraved on it. Dorothy has a marmalade cat named Pip.

Plane to Venice, Italy, seats 21 A+B, 8:10 p.m. (New York time)

(Boeing 763, 2-engine, wide-bodied plane, wingspan 156 ft. and 1 inch, seating capacity 229.) It's going to take us eight and a half hours to get there! But they have great things like peanuts and headphones and even flight attendants with press-on nails.

Plane to Venice, Italy, 7:00 a.m. (Venice time)

We're about to land at Marco Polo Airport. I can see Venice from the window! The streets are filled with water down there. Dorothy says they're called canals. She also says Venice is slowly sinking into the sea. I hope it doesn't sink while we're there!!!

Day One: Marco Polo Airport
I see Dorothy!!! We greet each other
Italian style: a kiss on both cheeks
(kiss = *bacio*). This takes a while.

On the vaporetto with M. and D. P. and P.

The oldest way to get around Venice is by *gondola*. These are long, skinny black boats, kind of like water limos. Imagine a gondola traffic jam at rush hour! But to get to Great Aunt Dorothy's, we're taking a *vaporetto*, which is like a boat-bus that drops people off at different stops. I feel like a pirate princess sailing the windy seas. After ten minutes we're at Dorothy's stop near the Accademia art gallery. There is even a gangplank!

At Dorothy's

Dorothy's doorway is not easy to find. There is no purple awning and no doorman. We have to wind our way up narrow steps to reach Dorothy's flat on the top floor of an old villa. Mmmmmm … her place smells of gingersnaps, my favorite.

Dorothy's salotto

Dorothy's living room, or *salotto*, is filled with art.
She fancies herself a bit of a collector.

She tells me she bought this Mitsukoshi years ago in New York for a song, which at the time was a lot of money. It requires regular dusting.

PORTRAIT OF
SELF WITH DOG
EARLY ZOE SOPHIA (PURPLE PERIOD)
CRAYON ON HEAVYWIEGHT BOND

My favorite is a large blue picture with green and purple animals that hangs over the fireplace. Dorothy tells me that the painting, which is by Chagall, was given to her by a Russian admirer named Boris many years ago in Paris. (Dorothy has gobs of unusual friends.) We have Chagalls in New York, too, I tell her. There are two giant paintings by him inside the Metropolitan Opera House. I've seen them myself.

I cannot believe it. Dorothy has framed my, YES MY, very own artwork. There is even a plaque.

La prima collazione, 10:00 a.m.

First off, we're having breakfast, *la prima collazione,* which means "the first meal." (Thank goodness—I'm starving!!!) We're having *cornetti,* a kind of croissant sprinkled with sugar on top (YUM!), and *spremuta,* juice. Dorothy has coffee, to get her eyes open, she says. Dorothy's dining room looks out onto the gondola repair shop. Dorothy says that gondolas frequently need touch-ups, just like people.

Back at Dorothy's, 9:00 p.m.

No time to write today!!! After breakfast, we went to the Accademia to look at HUGE paintings, and by the time we got out of the museum it was almost five o'clock! I never imagined I could spend a whole day just looking at paintings. My favorite was one by Tiepolo. He liked purple about as much as I do. Dorothy had a story to tell about each and every picture. Everything is fun with D. P.! She's even better than I imagined. I am working on a scrapbook.

Day Two

Today we went to the Laboratorio Artigiano Maschere—the mask shop. In Venice they have a festival every year in February called Carnevale, when people put on masks and capes and go into town all dressed up in costumes. Dorothy says they even ride around in gondolas in these getups! We tried on practically every single mask and cloak in the entire shop, but the saleswoman did not look too happy about it. Criminey!

Day Three

We went shopping on a bridge called the Rialto on top of the Grand Canal. Dorothy said it was built in 1590, back in the days of Italian princesses! They have everything there—mostly miniature plastic gondolas. I bought postcards for my new scrapbook. Dorothy says the money in Italy used to be called lire, but now they use euros. The coins have a big eagle on one side with stars all around. I used two of them to buy my postcards.

On the way home we took a gondola! The gondolier sang "La donna è mobile"—an aria from *Rigoletto*. He almost fell into the canal taking his bow. Dorothy said he must be a professional. He told us we should go to the opera at La Fenice on the Grand Canal.

Back at Dorothy's, 4:30 p.m.

Criminey! Something horrible has happened. Mickey is lost!! I was going to get him a dog treat, when I realized that he was nowhere to be found. Dorothy said maybe we left him in the gondola. But come to think of it, HE WAS NOT IN THE GONDOLA! Now we must retrace our steps *subito* (immediately). I have sketched a map, indicating all the places we went.

Pleaseohpleaseohpleaseohpleaseohplease, don't let him be gone!!!!!!!!!!!

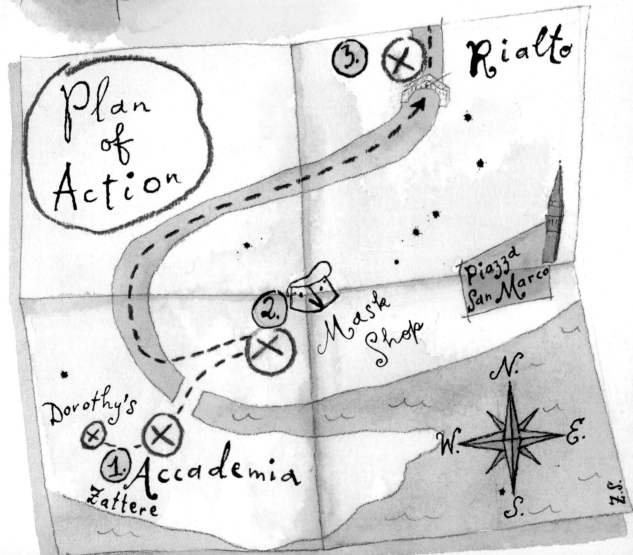

Plan of Action

③. ⊗ Rialto

Piazza San Marco

②. Mask Shop

Dorothy's ⊗

⊗ ①. Accademia

Zattere

N. W. E. S.

Later the same night

We've been all over Venice looking for Mickey. No Mickey. Now it is too dark to look any further. I can't sleep, even though Dorothy gave me milk and gingersnaps. What if Mickey fell into the canal? His doggie paddling is not up to snuff. All I can think about is poor Mickey out there all alone. He is afraid of the dark. He doesn't even speak Italian! We have only four days left before our flight back to New York! That is four days to find Mickey. I will never get to sleep. What if I don't find him?

P.S. I knew I should have signed Mickey up for that canine survival class on West 86th St.

Day Four: Dorothy's

Things are looking really bad. *(Orribile!)* We went to the animal shelter first thing this morning. NO MICKEY. Pip had the nerve to pick up a kitten there. CATS! Now I am really scared. Dorothy keeps saying don't worry. She typed up a notice with *ricompensa*, which is "reward," in big letters on it. She says we must post signs all over Venice, but it's pouring rain. So she is cooking us lunch first, *spaghetti al nero*, which is spaghetti made black with squid ink, to cheer me up. Sounds kind of yucky, but Venetians love it, Dorothy assures me. We'll see ...

Trovato! Found!

You won't believe this! We are having spaghetti al nero (which turns your mouth black too) when the doorbell rings. It's our gondolier, Ludovico! He's soaking wet and holding—guess who—MICKEY. He saw Mickey's silver tag with "New York" on it and bingo! He realized he must be mine. He's also holding a brown dachshund named Aïda. Mickey licks me all over and eats a whole dish of spaghetti al nero.

Naturally, we invite Ludovico to eat with us while his wet socks hang over the tub to dry. *"Grazie mille!"* we say, which means "thanks a million!" Ludovico is grand. He's giving me his e-mail address and promises to get Dorothy online as well. Dorothy calls him *tesoro,* which means "treasure." She's inviting all of us to the opera at La Fenice tonight to celebrate. I AM SO EXCITED!!! I love Venice! *Bella Venezia!*

La Fenice

The opera was *La Traviata*. Dorothy wore her beads from Botswana. Ludovico had on a tux! It was so *fantastico* that Dorothy cried the whole time. Mickey and Aïda had their own loge, thanks to a friend of Dorothy's who is on safari in Africa. Pip brought his date, the kitten, who is named Camille and who is not so bad. I cried too, a little, but mostly because I have only two more days left in Venice and I'm having such a good time here. Tomorrow Dorothy is taking me to a Venetian glass factory!

Day Five: Murano, Maestro Domenico Tagliatelle Glassblowing Studio

We got up early and took a boat to the island of Murano, which is world-famous for glassblowing. An old friend of Dorothy's, Domenico, is a master glassblower. His family has been in the business since the thirteenth century. Domenico can make anything from a chandelier to a paperweight, and he's not afraid to blow through a pipe with red-hot glass on the end. But his favorite thing is making beads by slicing colored glass rods. Each bead has a tiny flower in it, and no two are ever alike. This technique is called *millefiori*, which means "a thousand flowers." I finally chose a millefiori paperweight to bring back to my teacher, Ms. Feinschmecker. It weighs a ton.

Day Six: Piazza San Marco, feeding pigeons

We've been feeding the pigeons in front of the Basilica San Marco, which is the thing to do in Venice. This cathedral is named after Saint Mark, who is the patron saint of Venice. His symbol is the lion, and there are lion sculptures absolutely all over town. I've counted fifty-three, so far.

Dorothy explains that pigeon droppings are a huge problem in Venice. Luckily, she has brought an umbrella. Besides, it is starting to rain.

Caffè Florian's, having hot chocolate

We are soaked. We have come to warm our insides in Caffè Florian on the Piazza, which serves the best hot chocolate in town. According to Dorothy, Venetians have come to Florian's since 1720. The rooms are tiny. It's like we're sitting inside our own private jewel box lined with mirrors and paintings. The hot chocolate is so thick the spoon practically stands up in the cup by itself.

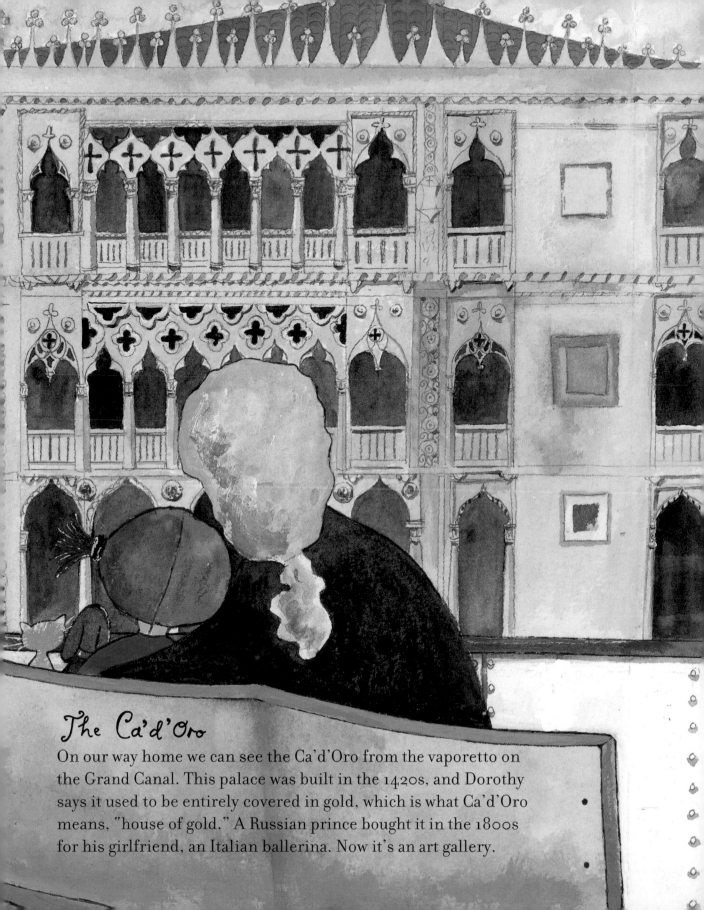

The Ca'd'Oro

On our way home we can see the Ca'd'Oro from the vaporetto on the Grand Canal. This palace was built in the 1420s, and Dorothy says it used to be entirely covered in gold, which is what Ca'd'Oro means, "house of gold." A Russian prince bought it in the 1800s for his girlfriend, an Italian ballerina. Now it's an art gallery.

One flask
Passione Primavera
perfume for
my mother

One box Accademia
pencils for myself

One gondola
pencil sharpener
for my
friend Alexa

Day Seven: at Dorothy's, packing

I am majorly bummed that we have to fly home tomorrow. Dorothy promised that tonight, when I finish all my packing, she will take me to Quadri's, Venice's finest restaurant, so we can dine in style on our last evening. YUM!

Here is what I bought for everyone back home:

One millefiori paperweight for my teacher, Fionnula Feinschmecker

One pair leather driving gloves for my father, who travels a lot

One package Venetian dog treats for Mickey

One mustache-trimming kit for Victor Gonzales, my doorman

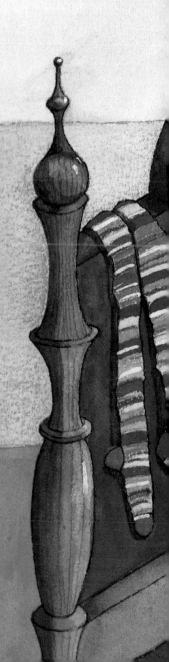

— One art portfolio (for me)

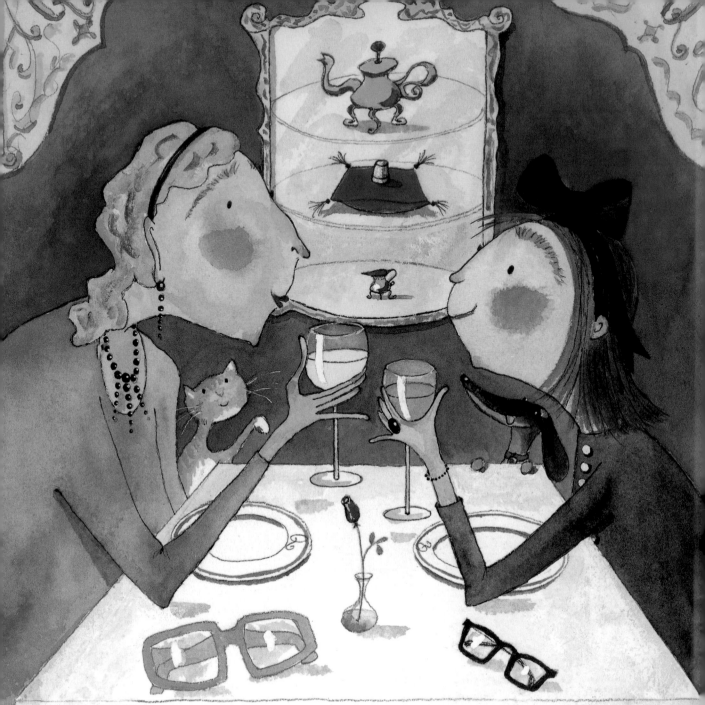

Quadri's

I am having *farfalle al pescatore* (seafood bowtie pasta) with a side order of fries. Dorothy is sticking with her usual fish, *sogliola* (filet of sole). Dorothy has big news! Her manuscript has been accepted by her N.Y. publisher, Peter Winsome. This means that she will fly over in the spring for a book tour, and maybe I can go along! YAY!!!!!!! We order *tiramisù* for dessert, which means "pick me up."

Later

After dinner, we walked across the Piazzetta in the moonlight. Dorothy said it takes her breath away. Mine too. I get all choked up when I think about saying *arrivederci* (good-bye) to Venice, and Mickey's nose is all dry, which is how it gets when he is trying not to cry.

Ciao Venezia!

Ludovico taught Dorothy how to use e-mail, so now we can send messages to each other every day. Dorothy is right, Ludovico is a tesoro. He gave Mickey a locket with Aïda's picture inside to wear on his collar and me a picture of himself in his gondola for my scrapbook.

Tomorrow, Mickey and I will be back on the plane to New York. I am sad to leave, but also kind of excited about showing my scrapbook and sharing our adventure with everyone back home. But for now, I am *esaurita*, which is totally pooped. *Buona notte!* Good night!

P.S. Mmmmm…my pajamas smell like gingersnaps now too!

Ciao for now.

Venezia

vaporetto tickets

Dorothy, checking her chives

world's best gondolier!

typical gondola